From Farm to Store

by Wallace Boten

Reading Consultant: Wiley Blevins, M.A.
Phonics/Early Reading Specialist

 COMPASS POINT BOOKS

Minneapolis, Minnesota

Compass Point Books
3109 West 50th Street, #115
Minneapolis, MN 55410

Visit Compass Point Books on the Internet at *www.compasspointbooks.com*
or e-mail your request to *custserv@compasspointbooks.com*

Editorial Development: Alice Dickstein, Alice Boynton
Photo Researcher: Wanda Winch
Design/Page Production: Silver Editions, Inc.

Library of Congress Cataloging-in-Publication Data
Boten, Wallace.
  From farm to store / by Wallace Boten.
      p. cm. — (Compass Point phonics readers)
Summary: Discusses how peanuts are grown, harvested, and processed into
peanut butter in an easy-to-read text that incorporates phonics
instruction.
Includes bibliographical references and index.
  ISBN 0-7565-0507-0
  1. Peanut butter—Juvenile literature. 2. Reading—Phonetic
method—Juvenile literature. [1. Peanut butter. 2. Peanuts. 3.
Reading—Phonetic method.] I. Title. II. Series.
  TP438.P4B67 2003
  664'.8056596—dc21   2003006351

Table of Contents

Dear Parent or Caregiver,

Welcome to Compass Point Phonics Readers, books of information for young children. Each book concentrates on specific phonic sounds and words commonly found in beginning reading materials. Featuring eye-catching photographs, every book explores a single science or social studies concept that is sure to grab a child's interest.

So snuggle up with your child, and let's begin. Start by reading aloud the Mother Goose nursery rhyme on the next page. As you read, stress the words in dark type. These are the words that contain the phonic sounds featured in this book. After several readings, pause before the rhyming words, and let your child chime in.

Now let's read *From Farm to Store*. If your child is a beginning reader, have him or her first read it silently. Then ask your child to read it aloud. For children who are not yet reading, read the book aloud as you run your finger under the words. Ask your child to imitate, or "echo," what he or she has just heard.

Discussing the book's content with your child:
Explain to your child that peanut butter is a very popular food. Americans eat enough peanut butter in a year to make more than 10 billion peanut butter and jelly sandwiches.

At the back of the book is a fun Batter Up! game. Your child will take pride in demonstrating his or her mastery of the phonic sounds and the high-frequency words.

Enjoy Compass Point Phonics Readers and watch your child read and learn!

Little Boy Blue

Little Boy Blue, come blow your **horn,**
The sheep's in the meadow,
   the cow's in the **corn.**
Where's the little boy that looks after
   the sheep?
He's under the haystack, fast asleep.

Do you know how peanut butter is made? First a farmer buys peanuts. The farmer plants the peanuts in a big field.

Small green plants grow. Their branches bend over and go into the soil. Lots of peanuts grow at the end of the branches. These peanuts grow under the soil.

In the fall the farmer harvests
the peanuts. He uses a big tractor.
The farmer sells the peanuts
to a factory. He takes the peanuts
to the factory in trucks.

At the factory, a machine takes the shells off the peanuts. Then the peanuts are cleaned and roasted. It will take 850 peanuts to make 1 big jar of peanut butter!

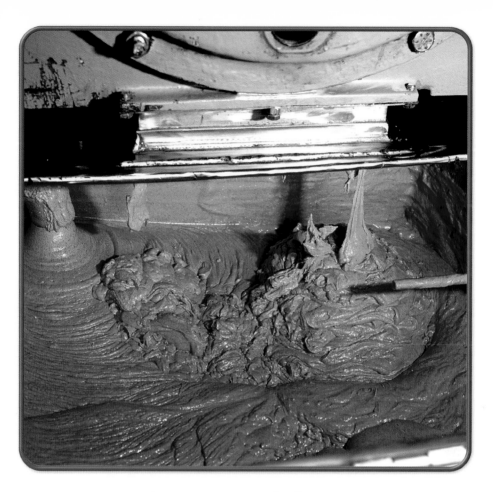

Machines grind the peanuts.
Then salt, oil, and sugar are
added to the peanuts. These four
things make peanut butter.

Machines pour the peanut
butter into jars. Lids are put on
the jars. Next the jars go to
stores. The peanut butter will be
for sale.

Lots of people like peanut butter. They buy jars and jars of it. Think of all the peanut butter sandwiches that can make.

Word List

r-Controlled Vowels *(or, ore, our)*

or
for
tractor

ore
store(s)

our
four
pour

High-Frequency
buy(s)
know
put
was

Social Studies
factory
machines
oil
salt
sugar

Batter Up!

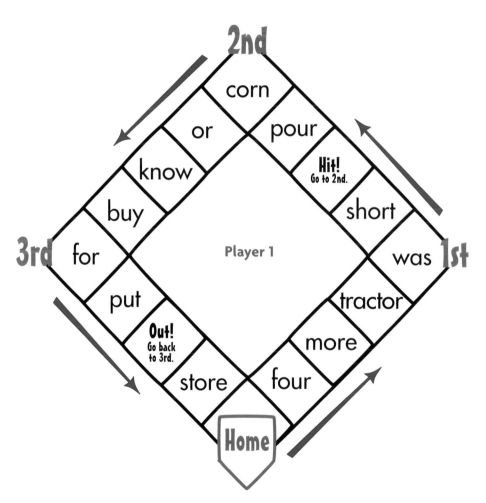

2nd

corn

or   pour

know   Hit!
Go to 2nd.

buy   short

3rd for   Player 1   was 1st

put   tractor

Out!
Go back
to 3rd.   more

store   four

Home

14

How to Play

- Put the moving pieces on Home. The first player shakes the penny and drops it on the table. Heads means move 1 space. Tails means move 2 spaces.

- The player moves and reads the word. If the child does not read the word correctly, tell him or her what it is. On the next turn, the child must read the word before moving.

- A run is scored by the first player to arrive at Home plate, and the inning is over. Continue playing out the number of innings previously decided. The player with the most runs wins.

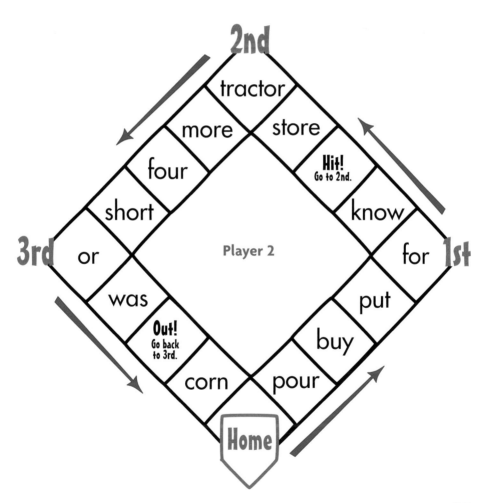

Read More

Hall, Margaret. *Peanuts.* Chicago, Ill.: Heinemann Library, 2003.

Hall, Zoe, and Shari Halpern (Illustrator). *The Apple Pie Tree*. New York: Scholastic, 1996.

Snyder, Inez. *Tomatoes to Ketchup*. How Things Are Made Series. New York: Children's Press, 2003.

Waters, Jennifer. *Harvest Time*. Minneapolis, Minn.: Compass Point Books, 2002.

Index

DATE DUE

DEC 1 9 2001	

BRODART, CO.   Cat. No. 23-221